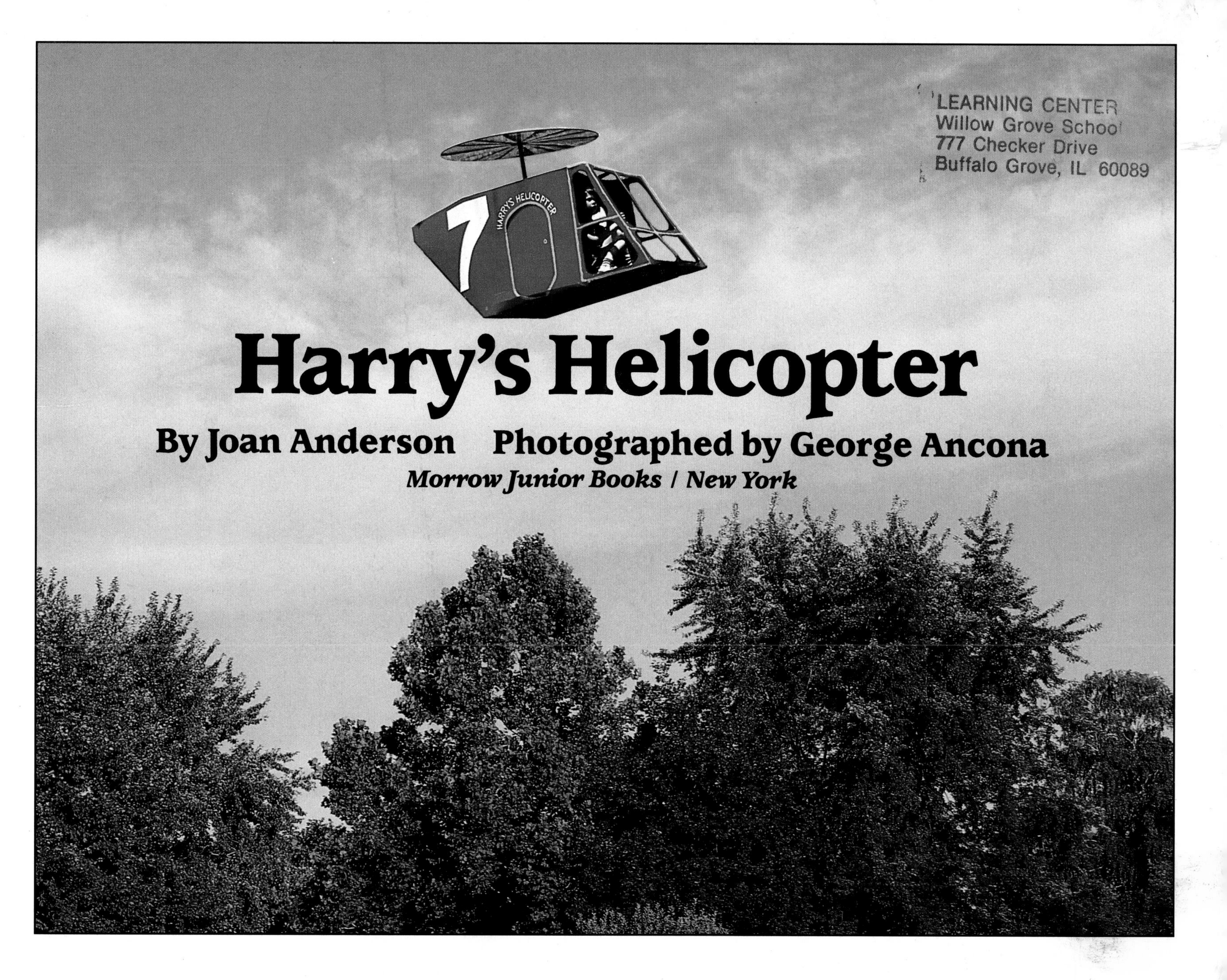

Harry's Helicopter

By Joan Anderson   Photographed by George Ancona

Morrow Junior Books / New York

ACKNOWLEDGMENTS

A big, giant thank-you goes to Ben Sloan, who played Harry Hopkins admirably. We are also grateful to the entire Sloan family for their participation in this project, and to Adelia and Charles Geiger for the use of their home and property in shooting this book. Others who made the project successful were the Good Humor Company of Nyack, Chaney Brand, Bettina and Anna Montano, David Bosch, Amy Onderdonk, and the balloon lady.

Joan Anderson
George Ancona

Inquiries should be addressed to
William Morrow and Company, Inc.,
105 Madison Avenue,
New York, NY 10016.
Printed in Singapore at TienWah Press.
1 2 3 4 5 6 7 8 9 10
Library of Congress Cataloging-in-Publication Data
Anderson, Joan.
Harry's helicopter/by Joan Anderson : photographed by George Ancona.
p. cm.
Summary: One day Harry's bright red cardboard helicopter takes off with him in a gust of wind and gives him a thrilling ride.
ISBN 0-688-09186-5.—ISBN 0-688-09187-3 (lib. bdg.)
[1. Helicopters—Fiction.] I. Ancona, George. ill. II. Title.
PZ7.A5367Har1990
[E]—dc20 89-28601 CIP AC

To John Emmerling

J.A.

This one's for Pablo.

G.A.

There was nothing Harry Hopkins liked better than helicopters. Every day after school, he would take one of his toy copters, head for the backyard, and fly it for hours. No place was too far away; no job was too hard for Harry and his helicopter.

On Harry's birthday, his father had a big surprise waiting for him. Sitting out on the back lawn, gleaming in the early-morning sunlight, was a bright red cardboard helicopter! And it was big enough for Harry to climb into.

"Can it fly?" Harry asked as he looked over his chopper from top to bottom.

"Knowing you, Harry," his dad answered, "I wouldn't be surprised."

7
HARRY'S HELICOPTER

From then on, Harry spent every spare moment in his helicopter. He pretended to take off, land, and to steer his chopper over and around obstacles, both big and small.

At the end of every flight, Harry would pat his helicopter and say, "Someday we'll take more than a make-believe trip. You'll see; one of these days we'll *really* fly."

HARRY'S HELICOPTER

One afternoon while Harry was flying his copter, a strong wind was blowing. Suddenly Harry heard a strange noise. Poking his head out the window, he saw his helicopter's blades spinning. *Whoosh, whoosh, whir,* they purred steadily. *Whoosh, whoosh, whir.*

"That's weird," Harry said out loud. "They've never moved before." Was the wind turning them?

Before he could stop wondering, the little copter started to rumble, and the control stick flapped back and forth like a happy dog wagging its tail. Next the chopper started to move—a few inches one way, a few inches the other.

And then it happened.

Harry's helicopter took off!

7
HARRY'S HELICOPTER

"Whoa!" Harry squealed, feeling excited and scared at the same time. "I can't believe it. We're in the air!"

Splut, splut, sput. . . the blades roared in reply.

In seconds Harry and his helicopter were hovering above the roof of Harry's house. In another minute they were flying up Main Street. People pointed, and traffic all but stopped as the red craft cruised by, dodging telephone wires and just clearing treetops.

Getting braver by the second, Harry pulled back on the control stick, and they soared up even higher. "Wow!" he exclaimed, feeling like a balloon that had just escaped from its owner's hand.

In every direction there was endless blue sky. "I've got enough room up here to see just what my helicopter can do," Harry thought. And without a moment's delay, he pushed down on the control stick.

"Oh, no!" Harry roared, his stomach doing flip-flops as they dived down toward the treetops. He pulled back on the stick and leveled the craft. "I didn't mean for us to land so quickly."

After his heart stopped pounding, Harry eased the stick to the right and the left, and the little helicopter glided gently in each direction. "That's better," Harry said, proud of his cardboard copter's flying skill.

7

"So this is what a bird's-eye view is." Harry chuckled, gazing down on a church steeple and zooming past a radio tower.

Suddenly his earphones began to crackle. "Tower to Harry. Tower to Harry. Report your direction."

"Huh?" Harry murmured, stunned to hear the voice. Until then he hadn't even thought about where he was going. "Heading east toward the river," he answered, deciding that was as good a way to go as any.

"All right, then," the voice answered. "Fly carefully. Over and out."

"It sure is quiet up here," Harry noticed, "and kind of lonely, too." He was beginning to wish he was back in his yard when two sea gulls appeared at his side and peered in at him. Harry stared back. Suddenly the birds flapped their wings, dived in front of the helicopter, and circled once, seeming to beckon Harry to follow.

"Why not," he thought, shifting the control stick to the left and taking off after them. "They know this sky better than I do."

Together the birds and the copter soared, up and down, side to side, dipping and turning like three acrobats as they headed south.

Harry was having so much fun that he forgot to look where he was going. "Oh, no!" he gasped when, out of nowhere, a giant bridge loomed in front of him.

There wasn't enough room to fly under it! "We'll have to go over the top," Harry decided. "But can we do it in time?" He yanked the stick toward him. The copter whined and spluttered as it strained to climb higher and higher. "C'mon," Harry coaxed as the bridge came closer and closer.

Plink, plinkity, plink, the little craft answered. And seconds later, it skimmed the top of the bridge's silver-colored arch.

But there was no time to relax. On the other side of the bridge loomed the city, just waiting to be explored.

"Wowee!" Harry shouted, not quite believing his eyes. From his vantage point, he felt bigger than the whole world. "So, what do we do now?" he asked his little copter. "Before anything else, I think we should find someplace to eat. I'm hungry. Let's see if we can touch down and get some food."

Beyond the tall buildings, the church spires, and the rows of crowded streets, Harry spied a huge park. "And that might be just the place," he decided.

Cruising closer, he saw sunbathers and baseball players on the lawn, and a small lake dotted with rowboats. He circled lower and lower until he found an empty spot, and landed *kerplunk,* right next to an ice-cream truck.

Before he knew it, he was surrounded by children.

"Where did you come from?" one boy asked.

Harry shrugged his shoulders. "From up north," he answered.

"How did you make this thing fly?" a girl wanted to know.

"It's a secret," Harry replied. But her question made him sort of nervous. He didn't know how he had gotten up in the first place, so how would he take off again?

SLOW CHILDREN
Ice cream
PITCH IN!
7
HARRY'S HELICOPTER

A gust of wind blew and Harry remembered—that's how it had all started. He ran and jumped into the pilot's seat. Clutching the control stick and wishing hard that he would take off, it happened. *Whoosh.* Another gust and they were flying again!

Up, up, and away from the grass and trees and people the helicopter flew. As they entered the maze of office buildings, Harry could see the shadow of his helicopter. How big it looked!

For a while Harry had fun peeking into windows and seeing the crowds of people below. But as he turned up one street and down another, he realized he didn't know where he was or how to get out. If he could see the river, it would lead to home; but the skyscrapers were blocking his view.

And then he heard the voice. "Tower to Harry. Tower to Harry. Where *are* you going?"

"Home," Harry cried. "I'm trying to go home."

"Well, get going, then. Over and out."

There seemed to be an opening straight ahead and a patch of sparkling blue beyond. Harry headed for it. He guided his little helicopter around a corner—and came face-to-face with an enormous head.

"Why, it's the Statue of Liberty!" Harry said, gaping at the huge figure. He'd never seen it from this close before. He steered his copter nearer for a better look. He circled and circled until the voice interrupted again.

"Harry, you said you were heading home."

"You're right, sir," Harry replied. "I'm on my way."

Before Harry knew it, he was flying past the radio tower, up his street, and landing, *kerplunk,* in his backyard.

"Phew!" he sighed, climbing out of the chopper. "We made it." Harry gave his little copter a thank-you pat and ran to the porch, where his father was reading the paper. "You'll never believe what happened to me today," Harry said breathlessly.

Harry's father put down the paper and looked at him. "Maybe I will," he said with a smile. "Tell me about it."

And Harry did.